FOLK·TALES·&·FABLES·OF
ASIA &
AUSTRALIA

FOLK·TALES·&·FABLES·OF ASIA & AUSTRALIA

Robert Ingpen & Barbara Hayes

CHELSEA HOUSE PUBLISHERS
New York • Philadelphia

First published in the United States in 1999
by Chelsea House Publishers

First Printing
3 5 7 9 8 6 4 2

Text Editor Molly Perham
Editor Diana Briscoe
Art Director Dave Allen
Editorial Director Pippa Rubinstein

ISBN 0-7910-2757-0

Typeset in Bookman.
Printed in Italy

Contents

Asia

1 Baba Yaga and the Stepdaughter 12

2 Baba Yaga and the Brave Youth 16

3 Momotaro or the Peach-boy 21

4 The Leather Bag 28

5 The Bridge of Magpies 35

6 The Son of the Ogress 38

7 The Prawn that Caused the Trouble 44

8 The Deceitful Pelican 49

9 Into the Jungle 54

Australia and New Zealand

10 How the Dingo Came to Australia 62

11 How the Sun Was Made 66

12 The Firemakers 69

13 Wireenum the Rainmaker 73

14 Rainbow Serpent 76

15 Deereeree and the Rainbow 81

16 Maui, the Fisherman 83

17 Kahukura and the Fishing Nets 88

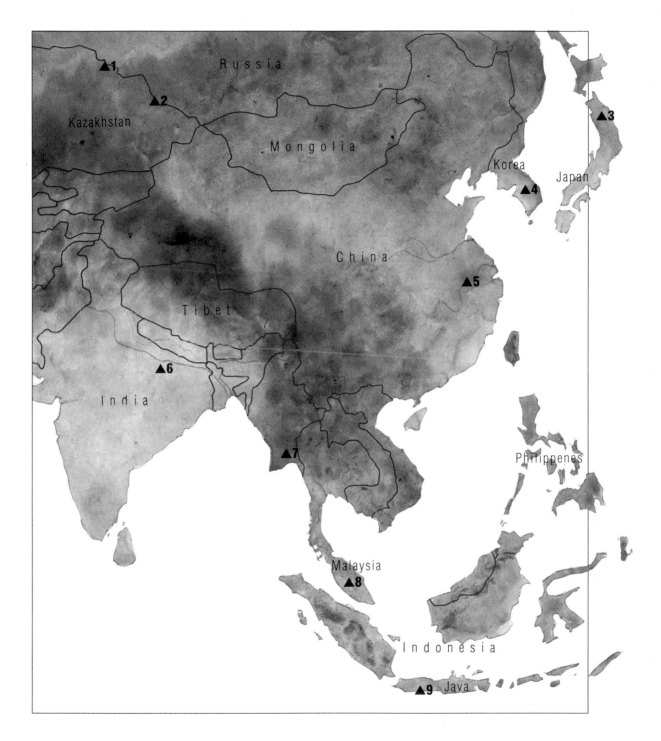

Asia

1 Baba Yaga and the Stepdaughter

2 Baba Yaga and the Brave Youth

3 Momotaro or the Peach-Boy

4 The Leather Bag

5 The Bridge of Magpies

6 The Son of the Ogress

7 The Prawn that caused Trouble

8 The Deceitful Pelican

9 Into the Jungle

1

Baba Yaga and the Stepdaughter

Russia was once a poor country of peasant farmers, ruled by tsars, or emperors. Books were devoted almost exclusively to church matters, so folktales were passed on by storytellers. They were not written down until the nineteenth century. Then a man named Afanas'ev made a great collection of all the folktales he could trace.

A peasant girl named Karen lived with her parents in a cottage at the edge of the forest. Karen was only twelve years old when her mother died. Her father married again, but his new wife hated her young stepdaughter. A few months after the wedding the father went away to visit friends, and the new wife saw her chance to get rid of Karen.

'Would you run an errand for me?' she said. 'Go and visit my sister, who is now your Aunt Irena. Ask her to give you a needle and thread to make a shirt.'

Instead of giving directions to the Irena's house, the wife told the girl the way to the house of Baba Yaga, the witch. Karen guessed that her stepmother intended harm to come to her, so she went first to the home of her real aunt.

'Hallo, my dear little niece,' the aunt said. 'Why have you come to visit me?'

'My stepmother has sent me to visit her sister, Irena, to ask for a needle and a thread to sew a shirt. But I think that something bad will happen to me,' replied Karen.

The aunt asked what directions the stepmother had given. When she heard where Karen had been sent she said, 'That is a dreadful place. A birch tree will lash your face; here is some ribbon to tie up the branches with. The gates will creak and not let you through; here is oil for their hinges. Dogs will try to tear you to pieces; here is some bread to throw to them. A cat will try to scratch out your eyes; you must give him this ham.'

'Thank you, Aunt,' said Karen and went on her way. Eventually she came to a house that she thought was Irena's, but was really the home of Baba Yaga.

'Good afternoon, Auntie,' said Karen to the skinny-legged woman sitting inside the house. 'My stepmother has sent me to ask for a needle and thread to make a shirt.'

Baba Yaga, seeing a plump girl who would make a tasty supper standing there, was careful to say nothing that would drive her away.

'Did she, dear? Then come in and sit down,' Baba Yaga smiled. 'I will give you the needle and thread in a moment, but first I would like you to do a little work for me.'

Baba Yaga told Karen to begin weaving at the loom that stood in the corner. Then she hurried out to her maid.

'My niece has arrived on a visit.' she said. 'Heat some water to give her a good wash. Wash her well, because tomorrow I want to eat her for my breakfast.'

Karen was terrified when she heard these words, but she managed to keep her wits about her. When Baba Yaga went out, Karen said to the maid, 'You are burning too much wood. Pour some water over it to cool it down. But do not bring too much water or you will put the fire out. Bring the water in a sieve.'

Karen gave the maid her scarf as a present. No one had ever given her a present before, so the maid did what Karen told her and went about her work extremely slowly.

A cat came into the room spitting and scratching. Karen gave it the ham and asked, 'How can I escape from this place?'

The cat gave Karen a towel and a comb. 'Run away,' he said. 'Baba Yaga is sure to follow you, so keep putting your ear to the ground. When you hear the thud of her footsteps, throw down the towel and a wide river will appear.

'If Baba Yaga is very hungry, she will cross the river and continue to follow you. Keep putting your ear to the ground, and when you hear the thud of her footsteps for the second time, throw down the comb and a thick forest will spring up. Baba Yaga will stop chasing you and will return home.'

Karen thanked the cat and, taking the towel and the comb, ran out of the house. The dogs in the yard stared at her with their tongues hanging out. As she passed them they barked at her heels, and seemed about to tear her to pieces. Karen threw them the bread her aunt had given her and the dogs let her pass.

As she reached the gates they slammed shut. Karen poured the oil on to their hinges and they swung open again and let her through.

A birch tree lashed its branches across the path in front of her. Karen took out the ribbon and tied back the branches.

Meanwhile Baba Yaga returned home. She stood at the door and called, 'Dear little niece, are you working hard at the weaving?'

The cat, who had been pleased with the gift of ham, tried to help Karen. He pushed and pulled at the loom and replied, 'Yes, Auntie. I am working hard.'

Baba Yaga was not so easily fooled. The loom was not making the correct noise and the cat's voice was harsh, not soft like Karen's. Baba Yaga rushed into the room. Seeing that Karen was gone, she beat the cat and shouted, 'Why have you turned against me?'

'In all the years I have served you, you never gave me ham, but that girl did, so I helped her,' said the cat.

Flinging the cat into the corner of the room, Baba Yaga ran into the yard and started to whip the dogs. 'The girl must have run through this yard. Why did you not tear her to pieces?' she shrieked.

'In all our lives, you have never given us so much as a burned crust,' snapped the dogs. 'But that girl gave us some bread, so we helped her.'

Then Baba Yaga started to kick the gate. 'You let a fine

breakfast through,' she screamed. 'Why did you not keep the girl locked in?'

The gates swung easily on their comfortable oiled hinges. 'You let us rust, but she gave us oil, so we let her through,' they murmured.

Baba Yaga ran through the gates and glared at the birch tree, preening itself in its pretty ribbon. 'Such vanity!' she snarled. 'I suppose that wretched girl gave the ribbon to you.'

'Indeed she did,' rustled the birch. 'Is it not beautiful? You have never given me so much as a piece of string to stop my branches from blowing into tangles. Of course I let the charming girl through.'

The maid leaned from a window of the house and shouted, 'The girl gave me this pretty scarf and I helped her too. You should treat us better, if you want us to be faithful.'

'What a pretty trouble-maker that girl has turned out to be,' screeched Baba Yaga. 'She must not live a day longer.'

Baba Yaga ran along the road in Karen's tracks. Far ahead, Karen put her ear to the ground and heard the thud of footsteps. She threw the towel on the ground between herself and Baba Yaga and at once a broad river appeared.

Karen ran on, hoping that she would hear no more footsteps. But Baba Yaga was so angry that she would not be stopped by a river. When she stepped into the water the heat of her anger turned it to steam, so she walked easily to the other side.

Again Karen put her ear to the ground and heard the thud of Baba Yaga's footsteps. She threw down the comb and, as the cat had said, a thick forest sprang up between them. This time Karen was able to hurry safely on her way. Baba Yaga spent several hours trying to push her way through the forest, but eventually she gave up.

When Karen finally arrived home she found that her father had returned from his journey. She told him what had happened to her and he was so angry with his second wife that he turned her out of the house. Karen never saw her stepmother nor Baba Yaga again. She married a nice young man and lived happily ever after.

2

Baba Yaga and the Brave Youth

Once upon a time a cat, a sparrow and a brave youth lived together in a hut in the forest. One day they ran short of firewood and the cat and the sparrow went out to cut logs. Before they left, they said to the brave youth, 'If Baba Yaga comes to count the spoons, keep quiet, or she will get you.'

'Very well,' agreed the brave youth.

A little later on, while the brave youth was dozing on the stove behind the chimney, Baba Yaga came into the hut and started to count the spoons.

'This is the cat's spoon and this is the sparrow's spoon and this spoon belongs to the brave youth,' she said.

The brave youth woke up and, feeling indignant that Baba Yaga was meddling with his spoon, forgot his promise. He shouted out, 'Baba Yaga, leave my spoon alone.'

At once Baba Yaga seized the youth, straddled the kitchen mortar as if it were a horse and urged it on with its pestle. As she rode out of the hut she snatched up a broom and used it to sweep away her tracks as she rode through the forest.

The brave youth shrieked at the top of his voice, 'Cat, run! Sparrow, fly! Save me from Baba Yaga!'

Hearing his cries the cat ran to scratch at Baba Yaga's legs and the sparrow flew to peck at Baba Yaga's eyes. And so the brave youth was saved.

The next day the cat and the sparrow again went into the forest to cut wood. 'We are going far away today,' they said to the brave youth. 'If Baba Yaga should come, be sure to keep quiet, for we will not be here to save you.'

'Very well,' agreed the brave youth. He sat down to keep warm on the stove behind the chimney.

Almost at once Baba Yaga entered the hut and started to count the spoons. 'This is the cat's spoon,' she said. 'This is the sparrow's spoon and this spoon belongs to the brave youth.'

Once more the brave youth was so cross that Baba Yaga was

touching his spoon, that he could not stop himself from calling out, 'Baba Yaga! Leave my spoon alone!'

Seizing him from the top of the stove, Baba Yaga started to drag the youth away through the forest. But he screamed, 'Cat, run! Sparrow, fly! Save me from Baba Yaga!'

Fortunately the cat and the sparrow had not gone far on their way. They heard the brave youth and returned. The cat scratched at Baba Yaga's legs and the sparrow pecked at her eyes, and they saved the youth as they had done the day before.

On the third day the cat and the sparrow again left to cut wood in the forest. Before they left, they once more warned the brave youth that, if Baba Yaga came into the hut to count the spoons, the youth must keep silent.

'We are going far, far away today,' they said, 'and if Baba Yaga gets you, we shall never hear your cries for help.'

When the cat and the sparrow had left the hut, the brave youth again sat on the stove behind the chimney to keep warm. There was no sound of Baba Yaga for an hour or more, but at last she came into the hut and started to count the spoons. 'This is the cat's spoon and this is the sparrow's spoon, and this spoon belongs to the brave youth,' she said.

Although the brave youth was furious that Baba Yaga was touching his spoon, he kept silent because he knew that the cat and the sparrow were too far away to help him.

Again Baba Yaga counted the spoons, saying, 'This is the cat's spoon and this is the sparrow's spoon, and this spoon belongs to the brave youth.'

The brave youth was beside himself with rage, but still he said nothing.

A third time Baba Yaga counted the spoons. 'This spoon belongs to the cat,' she chuckled, 'and this spoon belongs to the sparrow, and this spoon belongs to the brave youth and a very nice spoon it is too. I think I will take it and use it to eat my soup.'

At that the brave youth could hold his tongue no longer. Jumping down from the stove, he shouted, 'Baba Yaga! Leave my spoon alone.'

Immediately Baba Yaga seized the brave youth and dragged him through the forest. Although he called, 'Cat, run! Sparrow, fly! Save me from Baba Yaga!' no one came to help him.

Baba Yaga took the brave youth home, locked him in the wood shed and said to her eldest daughter, 'I am going to fly to Moscow to visit friends. While I am gone, cook the brave youth for my supper.'

'Very well,' replied the
eldest daughter and lit the stove
to heat the oven.

When the oven was hot, she
fetched the brave youth from the
shed and told him to lie down in the
roasting pan. He lay down
with one foot on the
floor and the other
jammed against the
ceiling so that he
could not be moved.

'Not like that, stupid!' said the
eldest daughter.

'How then? Show me!' said the
brave youth.

He stood up and the eldest daughter
lay down in the roasting pan and curled
up neatly to fit into the oven.

'Like this,' she said.

At once the brave youth pushed her
into the oven and went back to
the wood shed.

After an hour or so
Baba Yaga returned from
Moscow, licking her lips and saying how much she was going to
enjoy her supper.

'Only if you enjoy the taste of your own daughter,' shouted the
brave youth.

When Baba Yaga saw the brave youth uncooked in the wood
shed, she was furious and called her second daughter to her.

'Roast this brave youth for my supper,' she ordered and once
more went out to visit friends in Moscow.

The second daughter built up the fire in the stove and, when
the oven was hot enough, she fetched the brave youth from the
wood shed and told him to lie down in the roasting pan. He lay
down with one foot on the floor and the other jammed against the
ceiling so that he could not be moved.

'Not like that, idiot!' snapped the second daughter.

'How then? Show me!' said the brave youth, getting up and
making way for the second daughter to lie in the roasting pan.

'Like this, stupid!' jeered the second daughter, curling up in the pan neatly, ready to fit into the oven.

At once the brave youth pushed the second daughter into the oven and sat down to wait for Baba Yaga to return. Presently she came rushing in, laughing and calling, 'Set my supper on the table. I am longing for some slices of roast brave youth.'

'Then you will be disappointed,' called the brave youth, 'for roast second daughter is all that can be set before you.'

'You wretch!' screeched Baba Yaga. 'I will eat you yet.'

She called her third daughter and told her to cook the brave youth for supper. The brave youth outwitted the third daughter in the same way as he had tricked her sisters.

Then he stretched out in the warmth of the kitchen and waited for Baba Yaga to return. Her rage knew no bounds.

'To think that, with three daughters, I have to cook my own supper!' she shouted. 'Oh well, if you want a thing done, do it yourself, as the old saying goes. At least if I cook the brave youth myself, I know he will be correctly cooked to my liking. I suppose this is all for the best.'

She built up the fire in the stove and, when the oven was hot enough, she took out the roasting pan and told the youth to lie on it. He lay down with one foot on the floor and one foot jammed against the ceiling so that he could not be moved.

'Not like that, imbecile!" screeched Baba Yaga.

The brave youth got up from the roasting pan. 'How then?' he asked. 'Show me!'

'Am I the only one who knows how to do anything correctly?' asked Baba Yaga, as she lay down on the roasting pan neatly curled and ready to fit into the oven.

'No,' laughed the brave youth. 'Your daughters knew as well.'

He pushed Baba Yaga into the oven and ran home. He told the cat and the sparrow how he had escaped.

'I know how to deal with Baba Yaga,' he laughed. 'I am a brave youth.'

20

3

Momotaro
or the Peach-boy

This is an old folk story from Japan. The Japanese people were isolated from the outside world for over 200 years and lived according to the Samurai tradition of loyalty and service. Everyone knew their place in society and respected those of higher rank. Children were brought up to fulfill their family duties and support their parents in old age.

Spring had come at last. The harsh winter air had turned soft, ready to welcome the summer. The fields were freshly green, and the branches of the willow trees shook their catkins across the silver river.

An old woman knelt beside the river washing clothes. Little minnows darted through the eddies of a shallow backwater, flashing silver in the clear water. Suddenly the biggest peach that the old woman had ever seen in her life came rolling down the middle of the river.

'I am sixty years old,' gasped the old woman, 'and this is the first time that I have ever seen a peach as large as this. What a fine supper it would make for me and my husband.'

The peach was in deep water that came from the melted snow of the mountains. The old woman could not reach it. Leaning towards the huge fruit, she called softly:

'Deep waters are cold, but shallows are warm.

'Leave the cold and come to the warm.'

At the sound of her voice the peach stopped rolling about in the strong spring currents and bobbed into the shallow backwater where the minnows were darting about. It bobbed right up against the old woman's hand. She picked it up eagerly and took it home on top of her pile of washing.

At supper time her husband came home from where he had been cutting grass in the mountains. The old woman ran to meet him and showed him the peach.

'How wonderful,' he said. 'I am hungry. Let's eat it at once.'

The old woman took out a chopping board and a knife and was just about to cut the luscious peach in half when a child's voice called out, 'Mother, wait!'

The peach fell apart and a fine, strong little boy jumped out.

The old couple were amazed and frightened.

'Don't be alarmed,' laughed the boy. 'You have often complained to the gods that you have no child. At last they have taken pity on you and sent me down to be your son.'

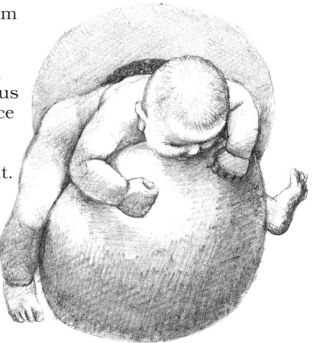

The old couple were delighted and, as the boy had come to them in a peach, they named him Momotaro, or Peach-boy.

The years went by and Momotaro grew up to be handsome, brave and immensely strong. One day he said to the old man, 'Father, my gratitude to you is higher than the mountains on which you cut grass and deeper than the river where my mother washes clothes. How can I ever repay my debt to you?'

'Don't thank us for doing our duty. Worthy people could do no less,' replied the old man. 'When we are old you will look after us, as is your duty, and you will owe us nothing.'

'It distresses me to leave you before my duty is done,' said Momotaro. 'But Father, will you give me permission to go away for a short while?'

The old man was surprised. 'Why do you want to leave your home? Where in all of Japan could you find more happiness than here?' he asked.

'In the north of Japan, separated from the mainland by a stretch of sea,' said Momotaro, 'is an island inhabited by demons. They do not obey the gods of Japan, but steal people and goods. I hope to kill them and bring their stolen riches back here. That is why I wish to leave you.'

The old man was astonished at this request. After deep thought, he realized that, as Momotaro had come from the gods, it was unlikely that they would allow any harm to come to him. He gave the young man permission to make the journey.

'If the demons are enemies of Japan, the sooner you kill them the better,' he said.

The old lady prepared Momotaro's clothes and made him some millet dumplings to eat on the journey. When he was ready to go, the two old people waved goodbye to him with tears in their eyes.

'Return victorious!' they called.

Momotaro walked quickly along the road, eager to get on with his task. At midday, he sat down at the side of the road to eat some of the dumplings. The scent of the food brought out a fierce dog that barked at his legs.

'You are on my territory. Give me some of your food or I will eat you alive!' he said.

Momotaro kicked the dog aside. 'Get away from me, you miserable cur,' he shouted. 'I am on my way to kill the enemies of Japan, but if you hinder me, I will kill you first.'

The dog cowered and trembled with fear. 'I see you are the mighty Momotaro,' he whimpered. 'I humbly beg you to forgive me. Please allow me to go with you to kill the enemies of our country.'

'I have no objection,' said Momotaro and gave the dog a dumpling.

As soon as they had finished eating, they went on their way through the high mountains. When they had travelled for many miles, a strange wild creature leapt down from a tree and stood in Momotaro's path.

'I hear you are the mighty Momotaro, marching to kill the enemies of Japan,' it said. 'Please allow me to go with you.'

At this the dog flew into a rage. 'What insolence!' he growled. 'You are only a mountain monkey. How dare you ask to go to war with Momotaro? I am the only one worthy enough to go with him.'

Naturally this speech made the monkey furious. He bared his teeth and was about to attack the dog with his sharp claws. Momotaro stepped between them.

'Don't be too hasty,' he said to the dog. 'This monkey could be useful. I want to take it with me as a companion.'

He gave the monkey half a dumpling and, when he had finished eating, they went on. However the monkey and the dog would not stop squabbling. There was no peace until Momotaro gave the monkey his standard and told him to march along the road ahead of them. He then gave his sword to the dog and

ordered him to walk behind. Momotaro himself held up his war banner and walked between the two of them.

So the little army marched on through the wilderness until a pheasant sprang up from the ground. The dog leapt forward, to eat the bird.

Momotaro stopped him and said to the bird, 'If you try to prevent me carrying out my mission, the dog will bite off your head. If you want to come with us, then you may become my companion.'

The bird bowed deeply and said, 'If you are the great Momotaro, whose fame has spread throughout the country, then may I, a mere pheasant, go with you to kill the enemies of Japan?'

The dog growled. 'Are we to be degraded by the company of this worthless bird?' he grumbled.

'That is not your decision,' replied Momotaro. 'I say that the pheasant can come with us and I warn all three of you now, that if there is any quarrelling, I will send you home. We will never defeat our enemies if we quarrel among ourselves.'

日本一

The three animals listened quietly and promised to obey Momotaro. The pheasant ate half a dumpling and became Momotaro's companion, and they all went forward together.

At last they came to the sea. They peered across the heaving waters but could see no island. The sea voyage would obviously be long and rough and the three animals trembled with fright.

Momotaro was disgusted. 'You cowards!' he cried. 'Are you afraid of the ocean? What sort of companions have I brought with me? I would have been better off alone. I will get rid of you now, as I should have done before. Go home!'

The three animals clung to Momotaro and begged to be allowed to stay. Believing that they had found some courage after all, he let them help him build a boat, and soon they were sailing across the wide ocean. The waters rose and fell. The animals felt ill and, to take their minds off their troubles, each animal showed off in its own way. The dog begged, the monkey performed tricks and the pheasant sang a mournful song. In no time at all they were at the island.

It was a fearsome sight. The path ashore was blocked by an iron gate. The houses were crowded together and protected by iron roofs. Flags flew defiantly in the wind.

Momotaro turned to the pheasant. 'Make use of your wings,' he said. 'Fly over the gate and see what these demons are doing on their fine island.'

The pheasant obeyed instantly and found all the demons sitting on their roofs. He called down to them, 'He who was sent by the gods, has come to destroy you. If you wish to save yourselves, surrender at once.'

'What vanity!' jeered the demons. 'Feel the edge of our weapons, pheasant, and give us no more talk of surrender!'

Rising up into the sky, the bird swooped down fiercely and pecked off the head of a red demon. Then, after a great struggle, the pheasant burst open the iron gate and Momotaro, followed by the dog and monkey, charged in.

The demons were very startled, for they thought the pheasant had meant itself when it spoke of the one sent by the gods. Their surprise at finding themselves attacked by four brave warriors made them fight all the more fiercely. But red and black and blue demons were soon falling to the ground, wounded and dying. Their screams drowned the sound of the waves on the rocks.

At last only the leader of the demons was left. Seeing that all his comrades had been killed, he threw down his weapons and broke off his horns as a sign of surrender. He knelt before Momotaro and offered him all the treasure of the island.

'Spare my life,' he begged, 'and I will never do wrong again.'

Momotaro laughed scornfully. 'You coward!' he cried. 'For years you have killed and robbed and now you talk of being spared. I will take you to Japan where your head will be cut off and stuck on a stake so that everyone may see that your reign of terror is over.'

So the monkey led away the chief of the demons as a prisoner. All the riches of the island were loaded on to the boat and Momotaro and his companions returned to Japan.

The old woman and her husband were overjoyed when their son returned to them victorious. And Momotaro looked after his parents until they reached a great old age.

4
The Leather Bag

The Korean Peninsula extends south from the land mass of Asia. To the east lies the Sea of Japan and Japan itself. To the west, across the Yellow Sea, is China. Korea is a mountainous country of forest and scrub, with farms near the coast and in the river valleys.
In the medieval period, when this story is set, farmers were prosperous, rich men who employed many servants.

An only son of rich parents lived long ago in the land of Korea. The boy loved listening to old fairy stories. Every evening a servant sat beside his bed and told him an exciting tale. Some of the tales were about fierce dragons and tigers; others were about bad fairies or the ferocious fox-spirits. Some were about good fairies and lovely maidens and gallant heroes.

An old leather bag hung on a hook on the boy's bedroom door. It had a tight drawstring round its neck, and as the servants told the stories, the spirits from the story had to go into the bag and stay there. They could come out again only when the boy told the same story to someone else.

Unfortunately for the story spirits, the young boy was very selfish. During the day, when he played with children of other families, they would say, 'We know your servants tell wonderful stories. Please tell some of them to us.'

The boy would not. He kept all the tales to himself.

As the years went by the old leather bag that hung on the hook on the door became more and more crowded. The story spirits, good and bad, were squashed together so that there was hardly any room to move. They became angry and discontented.

By the time the boy had grown into a youth there was only one storyteller left. This faithful old servant knew every old tale in the land. Although the boy was now almost a man, the servant still told him a new story every evening. Then yet another story spirit had to squeeze into the bag on the hook on the bedroom door.

'No room! We are squashed already,' shouted the spirits in the bag, but it was no use. Friends still asked to hear some of the many stories, but still the selfish boy refused.

The youth became a man. His parents died, but he had a kind uncle to watch over his affairs. As the young man was rich, the uncle had no difficulty in arranging a good marriage for him. All the preparations were made and the day arrived when the young man was to set out in procession for the house of his bride. The old servant, who was the storyteller, was about to enter the bridegroom's bedroom when he heard angry voices. He stopped, puzzled, because he thought the room was empty. Could he hear thieves? He crept forward quietly to listen.

'He's getting married today, you know,' said one voice.

'Yes,' added another, 'he is dressing up in grand clothes and going to a fine feast, but we are left in this crowded bag as usual.'

'It isn't good enough. We have been here far too long,' barked the unmistakable voice of a fox-spirit. 'Let's kill the selfish young man. When he is dead, we will be released from this bag.'

'What a good idea!' cried several voices.

'Yes, we will do that,' they agreed.

The old servant carefully pushed open the bedroom door and peeped at the old leather bag, hanging on the hook. To his surprise it was bulging and moving about, as the story spirits shook their fists and talked in angry voices. The spirits of the good fairies and lovely maidens and gallant heroes said nothing. They were afraid of the other spirits.

Fortunately for the selfish young man, the old servant loved him. He listened quietly as the story spirits went on with their plotting.

'It is a long ride to the bride's house,' said a tiger-spirit. 'The young man will become hot and thirsty. The water spirit is a friend of mine, so I will ask him to lurk in a well at the roadside and place a handsome gourd to float on the cool water. The young man will drink, then the water spirit can make him ill and choke him.'

'Wonderful!' laughed a fox-spirit. 'If that should fail by any chance, I will ask my friend, the strawberry fairy, to sit in a field beside the road. If the young man passes the well without drinking, he is sure to want to eat some ripe strawberries. My friend will jump down his throat with the berries and choke him.'

The leather bag swayed as the other spirits clapped and murmured approval.

Next the squeaky voice of a bat-spirit spoke. 'I know a bit about weddings,' he said. 'I know that when the bridegroom dismounts in the courtyard of the bride's house, a bag of rice husks is placed beneath his feet so that he can get down comfortably from his horse. I will arrange for a red-hot poker to be among the husks so that the young man is burned.'

'Oh, very good!' said all the other voices approvingly.

Then a snake-spirit hissed its contribution. 'I will ask a cousin to hide under the mat in the bride's bedroom,' he said. 'If everything else fails and the bridegroom joins the bride, my cousin will slip out from under the mat and bite him. That will be the end of all our problems.'

'Good! Good!' the story spirits laughed.

Then there was silence and the bag became still.

The old servant was horrified. He loved his master and wanted him to come to no harm. But he knew that if he told anyone this tale about the story spirits in the leather bag they would not believe him. They would think that he was mad.

'I must find another way of saving my master,' thought the servant. He went to see the uncle and asked permission to lead the young man's horse on the procession to the bride's house.

'Of course not,' replied the uncle. 'You are too old, the journey would be too far for you.'

'Please, please,' begged the old man. 'I have cared for my master for so long, I should like to take him to his wedding, then I will retire in peace.'

'Very well,' sighed the uncle. 'You may lead the horse.'

The wedding procession set out with the old servant holding the bridle of his young master's mount. The horse had an embroidered saddle and a bridle with tassels. The bridegroom wore magnificent clothes. There were attendants on foot. The uncle rode at the rear of the procession on a splendid horse led by a groom. Other servants led a beautiful horse-drawn litter in which the bride would ride on the return journey.

The sun shone down fiercely and, after riding for some distance, the bridegroom became thirsty. At that very moment he saw a cool well with a handsome gourd floating on the water. 'Fetch me a drink,' he ordered the servant.

The old man gripped the horse's bridle and hurried onwards. 'Now, young master,' he said, 'you must not stop for a drink. You know drinking in the bright sun will make you sweat and that will never do in your fine wedding clothes.'

The other attendants were amazed to hear the old servant contradict his master, but the procession went on.

Next they came to a field of strawberries. 'I am still thirsty and now I'm hungry too,' said the bridegroom. 'Fetch me some strawberries.'

'Now, master, you don't really want strawberries,' said the old servant, hurrying onwards. 'You will only drop juice down your fine outfit. You know that your dear mother never allowed you to eat while you wore your best clothes.'

The other attendants could scarcely believe their ears. They sent word back to the uncle that the mad old servant was refusing to obey his master. The uncle hurried forward.

'What is going on?' he asked. 'Is it true that this servant has refused to fetch a drink of water or any strawberries?'

'Yes, yes,' replied the bridegroom, 'but don't fuss. He is a faithful old servant.'

'There will be no fuss now,' the uncle fumed, 'but after the wedding, he will have a good beating.'

So the old servant took his master safely past the first two traps set by the story spirits and, in due course, the procession arrived at the bride's house. A great feast had been prepared and a large tent set up to shelter the guests. In the courtyard a sack of rice husks was placed at the side of the bridegroom's horse. As the young man dismounted, the old servant snatched the sack away.

'Have you really gone mad, old friend?' asked the young man, as he missed his footing and fell over. Again the uncle was furious and promised the servant a double beating, as soon as the marriage ceremony was over. The servant said nothing. He had saved his master from the third hazard.

Then the ceremony began. A cock and a hen, dressed in fine robes and tied to goblets of wine, were placed on an elegantly carved wooden table. Near the table was a lovely screen embroidered with dragons for good luck. The bridegroom stood to the east of the table. The bride, dressed in embroidered clothes and attended by two maidens, walked in from the west.

The bride and groom bowed to each other and took sips of wine from the goblets to which the cock and hen were tied. When the formalities were complete the happy couple greeted all their relatives and soon everyone was talking and laughing and enjoying the feast.

At last the time came for the bridegroom to retire with the bride to her chamber. This was the moment when the story spirits would make their last attempt to kill the young man. The old servant followed the procession to the bride's chamber door. Then, to everyone's astonishment, he pushed forward. He drew a sword from his clothes, lifted the rug and chopped to pieces the snake that lay underneath.

Such a fuss and commotion had never been seen in the household before. When the snake was dead, the old servant sighed with relief. All the plots to kill his young master had been foiled. Now he told the whole story of the spirits in the leather bag.

The young man believed the old servant and was sorry that he had been so selfish in keeping the story spirits squashed in the bag for such a long time. 'From now on I will tell to others the stories I have enjoyed so much myself,' he said.

In the course of time, children were born to the young man and his bride. Every evening the young man sat with his children and told them a story. They thought they had the best father in all the world.

One by one the story spirits were released to freedom and there was no more grumbling or evil plot-making. As for the old servant, he was not given a beating, but lived to an old age in a comfortable room next to the nursery.

5

The Bridge of Magpies

China is a land of ancient civilizations. This vast country covers an area of almost six million square miles, stretching from the Pacific Ocean in the east to the far borders of Tibet in the west. In the past Chinese merchants travelled to other countries and settled there. Here is one of the stories they took with them to Malaya, Myanmar, Java, Hawaii and many other countries. A similar story is also told in Japan.

Sometime, when you look up at the night sky, you may be lucky enough to see a silver river. This is the River of Stars that divides the northern skies from the southern kingdom of the heavens.

Long ago the King of the Land of the Stars had a beautiful daughter. This dutiful, hard-working girl sat every day at her loom weaving the clouds that floated across the skies.

One day a prince from a nearby kingdom rode near the palace of the King of the Land of the Stars. The Prince was inspecting his many horses and cattle. As he rode among the bellowing herds, the Prince looked towards the palace and saw the Princess sitting at a window, weaving. The Prince thought she was the loveliest girl he had ever seen, and asked for her hand in marriage.

The King of the Land of the Stars agreed to the match. 'My hard-working daughter deserves to marry a fine Prince with many cattle,' he said, 'and I am even happier because the Prince lives close to me. Though she is married, I shall still be able to visit my daughter and she can continue to weave the fleecy clouds that float through my starry kingdom.'

The wedding took place and the Princess went to live with the Prince in his palace. But so much for the plans of the King of the Land of the Stars! Marriage changed both the young lovers for the worse.

The Princess pushed her loom aside and wove no more clouds. She ran out into the sunshine and picked pretty flowers at the river's edge. She brushed her hair into different styles to please her husband and changed her clothes three times a day. She laughed with the dressmakers, asking for the prettiest new materials. She adorned her hands and neck with jewels.

'I have worked enough,' she laughed. 'Life is for enjoyment. There will be plenty of time for duty when I am old and grey.'

The Prince's behaviour was just as bad. He left the care of his lands and cattle to his servants. He laughed and danced with the Princess, and they spent their time idling among the flowers by the side of the river. When he was not with his wife, the Prince rode out with wasteful, frivolous friends. He decked himself out in extravagant clothes and gambled away his money.

'Why should I have to worry about cattle and rents and harvests?' he said. 'I must enjoy myself while I am still young and strong. Tomorrow may be too late.'

The King of the Land of the Stars was disappointed and angry. He needed clouds for his heavens. He did not want his daughter and his son-in-law reduced to poverty and dependent upon him. He was old and he had forgotten what it was like to be young.

The king sent for his daughter and her husband. 'You are not good for one another,' he said. 'You must be separated.'

He ordered his son-in-law to be banished to the north side of the River of Stars with his servants and horses and cattle. The Princess was ordered to stay on the south side of the river with her father and to resume weaving the clouds of the heavens.

The Princess wept and the Prince pleaded, but the King of the Land of the Stars would not relent. So the lovers were parted and they spent their days in misery and bitterness.

At last, seeing his daughter's unhappiness, the King of the Land of the Stars said, 'You may not be reunited with your husband, but I will allow you to go to the bank of the great River of Stars and gaze across and talk to your prodigal Prince.'

The Princess ran down to the river and, looking across the shimmering stars, she saw her beloved husband and called to him. He stood on the far bank and stretched out his hands towards his beautiful wife, but still the lovers were apart.

Their unhappiness was so great that their tears fell in a flood to the earth below. Fields and houses and trees were carried away by the torrents of tears.

Finally the birds met together to decide what should be done. After much twittering and chirping, the magpies offered to fly up into the heavens and form a bridge over the River of Stars.

'If the Prince and Princess are reunited and stop their weeping, then the earth will be saved,' they said.

All the magpies of the world gathered together into a whirling flock. They circled seven times around the tops of the trees, then flew up to the River of Stars. They gathered close together, head to tail, wings spread, and formed a swaying bridge from one side of the River of Stars to the other. The Prince and all his servants and horses and cattle crossed from the north to join the Princess in the southern heavens. By the time they had reached the other side, the heads of the magpies had turned black with the mud on the travellers' feet. To this day, those who look will see that the heads of magpies are black.

The Prince and Princess laughed with happiness. Their tears stopped flowing and the earth was saved. However, the King of the Land of Stars did not entirely forgive them.

'The magpies have taken pity on you,' he said, 'so they may continue to help you. On the seventh day of the seventh month of every year, the magpies may fly up to the heavens and make a bridge across the River of Stars. Then you may spend one day with each other. For the rest of the year you must stay apart, the Princess working at her loom and the Prince tending his estate.'

So it has been through all the centuries since. As the seventh day of the seventh month draws near, the Prince and Princess move to the banks of the River of Stars. On the seventh day of the seventh month, every magpie disappears from the earth and flies up to the heavens to make the bridge over which the Prince may travel to visit the Princess.

During the rest of the year, whenever rain falls heavily from the skies, the old people of China look up and say, 'The Princess is weeping with unhappiness.' On the seventh day of the seventh month no rain falls because the Prince and Princess are together.

6

The Son of the Ogress

The highways of old India were dangerous for an unwary traveller. As well as the tigers and poisonous snakes, there were bands of Thuggees, who worshipped Kali, the goddess of death. The Thuggees made friends with travellers by offering to ride with them as a protection against bandits. Then they strangled their victims at a chosen spot, robbed the bodies and buried them without trace. It is hardly surprising that legends grew up of monsters that lay in wait by the roadside.

India is a vast country and its roads are long and lonely. In the olden days travelling was dangerous because robbers and bandits lay in wait at the sides of the dusty highways, while ogres and angry spirits lurked in the forest glades and the mountain passes. Prudent people travelled in groups so that they could protect each other. Anyone who went alone had to be forever glancing over his shoulder.

It happened that a Brahman priest had to travel alone to Benares. A creature known as a Yakka lived in a cave near the side of the road. She had the body of a woman, but the head of a horse. She was wild and greedy and powerful and she lived by eating human flesh.

This terrible Yakka seized the Brahman and carried him to her cave intending to eat him, as she had eaten so many other unfortunate people. However, the man was young and very handsome and the Yakka fell in love with him. She said she would spare his life if he would marry her and live with her in the cave. The Brahman chose what seemed to be the lesser of two evils and agreed to marry the dreadful creature.

'Surely I shall find a way to escape soon,' he thought, 'and this nightmare will be over.'

The Yakka was very cunning. She never left the cave without rolling a huge boulder to block the entrance. The Brahman was a prisoner for several years. Shut up in the dark, damp cave he yearned to return to his life in the town.

It was true that the Yakka made every effort to improve her behaviour. Under the influence of the gentle Brahman, she gave up eating human flesh and ate fruits and grain instead. She drank wine instead of human blood. But she still lurked at the side of the road and robbed the caravans of travellers. She and the Brahman continued to live in the rough cavern, with its walls dripping with water, far away from the company of other people.

A baby was born to the Yakka. He was a beautiful boy. Fortunately, he took after his father. Both the Yakka and the Brahman loved him dearly.

One day, when the Yakka was out hunting, the boy said to his father, 'Why is my mother's face so different from ours?'

'Because your mother is an ogress and we are human men,' replied the Brahman.

Then the boy asked, 'Why do we stay in the dark of this damp cavern all the time when there is sunshine outside?'

'Because your mother is strong and will not let us leave. When she goes away, she rolls that huge boulder across the mouth of the cavern,' replied the Brahman.

'Why don't you push the boulder away so that we can escape?' asked the boy.

'The boulder is huge and I am not strong enough to move it,' replied the Brahman.

At that the boy smiled and, getting up, he put his young shoulder to the stone and rolled it aside easily. He was, after all, the son of his mother and had her strength.

Taking his father by the hand, the boy led the way out into the sunlight and the two of them hurried as fast as they could towards Benares. However, the sunlight dazzled them after their life in the darkness of the cavern. They stumbled and even the boy felt weak. Before long they heard the thud of the Yakka running behind them. She seized them both.

'My dearest son and my beloved husband,' she wept. 'How could you wish to leave me? Don't I work every day to give you everything you need? Don't I collect soft moss and ferns for your beds? Don't I bring wine, and dates for you to eat? Why are you running away?'

'Mother,' replied the boy, 'it is true that you bring us many delightful things, but we need light and air. Living in the dark is not good for us.'

'Very well,' agreed the Yakka, 'return with me and I will break the boulder at the mouth of the cavern. You may both go out in the sunshine and wander beneath the trees.'

Having little choice in the matter, the boy and the Brahman returned with the Yakka. She kept her promise and, from that day on, the man and the boy enjoyed the fresh breezes and the sunshine whenever they wished. But, whenever they went too far from the cavern, they heard the heavy thudding of the Yakka's feet behind them and they were dragged back to live obediently under her eye.

The boy, being the son of his mother, was able to learn her secrets. As he grew older, he came to know that the power of the Yakka reached only as far as the river in one direction, and for three leagues to the mountains in the other direction.

'Father,' whispered the boy one evening, 'do just as I say and tonight we will escape. I can no longer bear this lonely life away from other people.'

That night, when the ogress was asleep, the boy led the Brahman out of the cave. They ran as fast as they could and had reached the bank of the river before they heard the Yakka following them. The Brahman was exhausted, but the strong, young son picked up his father and carried him across the river to safety. Only then did he turn his head to look back.

The Yakka stood on the far bank and wept. 'How shall I live without you?' she cried. 'Come back to me!'

'Never!' called the boy. 'We are going to live in the land of humans.'

Then, realising that she had lost them forever, the Yakka called across the flowing river, 'My dear child, take this talisman to help you on your way through life. Hang it round your neck. Through its power you will be able to see footsteps made by men even though twelve years have passed.'

She threw a necklace with a stone pendant across the river. The boy picked it up and put it on. He thanked his mother and said goodbye to her. Then he and the Brahman turned away and never saw her again.

Happy in their new freedom, the father and son walked into Benares and went straight to the King's palace. There they asked to see the Grand Vizier.

The son of the ogress bowed and said, 'I have the power of seeing footsteps. Let me guard the King's treasure house. If any robber breaks in, I shall be able to follow his footsteps and retrieve the treasure. The King need fear thieves no more.'

The Grand Vizier gave this news to the King, who showed great interest and sent for the Brahman and his son. 'What do you want for guarding my treasure house?' he asked.

'He wants a thousand rupees a day,' replied the grand Vizier.

The King hesitated briefly. It was a lot of money. However, the treasure house was full of gold and jewels and the world was full of thieves. 'Very well,' agreed the King.

For some months the boy and his father lived happily at court, enjoying the company of men and the luxuries of palace life. No thief went near the treasure house because the tale of the boy who could see footsteps had spread through the land.

Then one hot day, as he sat longing for the touch of a cool breeze, the King said to the Vizier, 'I am restless at paying so much money to that boy. How do we know he really can see footsteps? He may be an impostor. Let us rob the treasure house ourselves tonight and see if the boy has the powers he claims.'

The Vizier agreed. That night he and the King broke into the treasure house, took several bags of gold and jewels, walked three times round the gardens and put the sacks in a tank of water.

The next morning they sent for the son of the Yakka.

'Boy,' said the King, 'the royal treasure house has been robbed. Now let me see you follow the footsteps and retrieve my riches.'

'Certainly, my lord,' smiled the boy. Wearing the necklace with the stone pendant given to him by his mother, he walked to the treasure house. There he clearly saw the footsteps of two men on

41

the ground. He followed them three times round the gardens and stopped at the tank of water.

'Send a man in here,' he said, 'and you will find the missing riches.'

Everyone clapped their hands as the sacks were taken from the bottom of the tank. They were impressed by the boy's magic powers.

However, the King was still displeased. He no longer wished to pay large sums of money to the boy.

'This is all very well,' he blustered, 'but anyone might have guessed that the tank of water was a good hiding place for stolen jewels. Can you find the thieves, my boy? That is the real test.'

As it happened, the Yakka's son had already recognized the footprints as those of the King and the Vizier, who naturally wore finer shoes than anyone else in the land. The boy hesitated to say who the thieves were, as it was shameful that two such noble men should be thieves and deceivers.

'Does it matter who the thieves are?' he asked. 'The treasure is regained. Surely that is the important thing?'

Now the King felt sure that the boy really had no magic powers and did not know who had taken the treasure. As he hoped to expose the boy as a fraud and so avoid paying him any more money, the King insisted. 'Find the thieves. They deserve to be punished. If you cannot follow the footsteps of the thieves and say who they are, I shall no longer pay you.'

Still the Yakka's son hesitated, for it is unwise to offend kings.

'The names!' jeered the King. 'Give me the names of the thieves or I shall have you declared a fraud.'

The boy pointed at the King and the Grand Vizier. 'You are the thieves,' he said. 'The footsteps lead to you.'

All the onlookers were shocked to learn that their respected ruler and the chief of his ministers could stoop to such trickery. Word spread through the city that the King and the Vizier were not fit to occupy positions of trust and respect. They were deposed and sent into exile, and the throne was given to the boy who was the son of an ogress.

7

The Prawn that Caused the Trouble

Myanmar lies on the eastern side of the Bay of Bengal. It borders India, Bangladesh, China, Laos and Thailand, and is dominated by the great River Irrawaddy that drains south into a vast delta.

Once, long ago, a man named Chemchongsaipa was standing on the banks of the River Irrawaddy, sharpening his weapons. A prawn, irritated by the stomping of the man's big feet as he moved around, bit him in the leg. That will teach him to come trampling about near me! thought the prawn, feeling rather pleased with himself.

The tall man could not see the small prawn so, in his anger at the stinging of the bite, he lashed out at a nearby tree and cut it. The tree was indignant. 'Why strike me, an innocent bystander?' it complained. The tree, intending to hit the man, dropped a piece of fruit as big as a melon from one of its branches, but it missed. The fruit landed not on the man, but on a cock that was unfortunate enough to be walking by.

The cock was not pleased, but he was afraid to attack the great tree so he scratched at a nest of ants. 'Everyone says you like work!' he squawked. 'Well, work to fix this damage. That should please you.'

The ants had enough work to do already and they resented the cock's sneering. 'Because we are good workers, everybody attacks us,' they complained. 'Jealousy is a terrible thing!'

The ants vented their anger by stinging a passing snake. 'Dear me! Dear me! In the wrong place at the wrong time!' sighed the snake. 'That is the story of my life!' He opened his mouth and darted forward to bite a boar.

'Why did you do that?' asked the boar.

'For the same reason that the ants stung me,' replied the snake, 'because you were there.'

Very few creatures care to argue with a snake. The boar

44

hurried off and took out his fury by rooting up a plantain tree.

A bat lived in the plantain tree, and he was not at all pleased at having his home flung to the ground. 'Someone will pay for this,' squeaked the bat. He blundered about until he flew into the ear of an elephant, and promptly bit it.

The elephant trumpeted with pain and kicked over a mortar that was used for pounding rice.

The mortar rolled down the hill and flattened the house that belonged to a little old lady. She was surprisingly fierce. 'Pay me the money to rebuild my house!' shouted the little old lady.

'Why should I?' screeched the mortar. 'It was the elephant who kicked me down the hill. He should pay for your house, which in any case should not have been in my way. You are lucky I do not ask you to pay me because of my bruises.'

The little old lady ran up the hill and confronted the elephant. 'Pay for my house to be rebuilt,' she demanded.

'Not I,' snorted the elephant, shaking the bat from his ear. 'Blame this bat, it is all his fault.'

'My fault!' squeaked the bat. 'How unfair! Can I help it if my home falls to the ground? Everyone should be rushing to my aid. If you have any complaints, go to that unreliable plantain tree.'

The plantain tree lay on the ground feeling very poorly. 'Blame the boar, not me,' it groaned. 'My roots are shrivelling up in the air and my head aches from my fall. Will you not stay to help and comfort me?'

'We all have our troubles!' snapped the little old lady. 'And I do hate to hear people whining. Stand up for yourself or be quiet!'

She chased after the boar. 'Give me the money to rebuild my house,' she said.

'Certainly not,' replied the boar. 'The fault lies with the snake who bit me.'

The little old lady took a forked stick and pinned the snake to the ground. 'Pay for my house to be rebuilt,' she said.

'Never,' spat the snake. 'I am completely innocent. I was harming no one until those ants stung me.'

'You snakes are untrustworthy,' said the little old lady. 'I will keep you prisoner until I have spoken to the ants.'

The ants admitted to stinging the snake, but said it was the fault of the cock who had driven them beyond endurance.

'Rebuild my house,' said the little old lady to the cock.

'Take your request to that tree, madam,' replied the cock. 'He dropped a large fruit on my head for no reason at all.'

'Is this correct?' snapped the little old lady to the tree.

'No reason at all!' gasped the tree, shaking with indignation. 'That man slashed me with a sharp weapon. Blame him for this!'

The little old lady felt quite cheerful. The man could do a fine job of rebuilding her house. As he was her son, she was sure that he would help. 'Rebuild my house,' she said to him.

'Very well, beloved mother,' he replied, 'but first I will get my own back on this prawn, who is the cause of all the trouble.'

The prawn looked around him, but could see nobody else to blame. He was indeed the cause of all the commotion.

The man, the tree, the cock, the ants, the snake, the boar, the plantain tree, the bat, the elephant, the mortar and the little old lady all stared down at the prawn. 'You deserve to die,' they said. 'Do you wish to die in cold or hot water?'

'In cold,' said the prawn and slipped away to the bottom of a pool, where he felt safe and happy. 'I fooled them!' he laughed.

He was not to enjoy the last laugh. All the creatures gathered round the pool and told the elephant to suck it dry. They seized the prawn and gave it to a toad to make into soup. The toad cooked busily and called the others to enjoy the feast. They began to eat but, after a moment, they looked at each other.

'This is water!' they complained. 'There is no taste of prawn.'

'Yes, well I am sorry about that,' sighed the toad. 'As I was making the soup I thought I would taste the prawn, to be sure it was cooked, and somehow I swallowed it. Accidents do happen.'

All the other creatures were so cross that they pinched the toad all over his back and that is why toads have warts on their backs to this day. Then the man rebuilt the home of the little old lady and replanted the plantain tree. Everyone agreed that although the soup was a disappointment, it had otherwise been an interesting day – for everyone except the prawn. No one asked his opinion.

8

The Deceitful Pelican

The Malay Peninsula stretches south from Thailand. To the east is the China Sea and to the west is Sumatra. People of many races came to trade and settle in Malaya, bringing their folktales with them. The Chinese told stories of their ancient land, the British brought stories from a cold country half a world away and the Polynesians brought legends from the vast Pacific Ocean. Meanwhile, the peasants of Malaya sat in their villages, in the half-light of the jungle, listening to the animal stories that had been told by the village storytellers for as long as anyone could remember.

The river tumbled from the mountains and slid over the edge of the rocks into a deep pool. The noise and turmoil made by the falling water was endless, or so Ruan the fish believed. Ruan did as his father had done before him, and as his grandfather had done before that, and as his great-grandfather had done before that. Ruan could think no further back than the days of his great-grandfather. He was not clever. Few fish are.

When he was not eating Ruan lay in the cool water at the bottom of the pool and tried to look like a mottled brown stone. His father had told him to behave so. His grandfather had told his father to behave so, and his great-grandfather had told his grandfather to behave so. None of them had ever wanted to do anything different. Fish are like that.

One morning a pelican came to stand by the side of the pool. The great pouch under his large beak was empty. For days the pelican had had little luck with his hunting; he was tired and hungry. He stared down into the pool and saw Ruan the fish lying on the bottom, pretending to be a mottled brown stone. The pelican was a solitary creature and liked to stand by himself and think. That day he was thinking up a cunning plot.

The pelican tossed his head and said, 'The creatures of this pool live in times of dreadful danger. How I admire their courage.'

At once Ruan the fish hurried up from the bottom of the pool, filled with curiosity. He forgot everything his father and grandfather and great-grandfather had said about pretending to be a mottled brown stone. Fish have few brains.

'Dear me! Dear me! What is this talk of danger?' he flapped. 'I have a young family to consider. Tell me what is wrong?'

The pelican looked down at Ruan with interest. 'You have a young family?' he asked. 'Tender little fishlets are they?'

'Oh, indeed, indeed!' agreed Ruan the fish. 'I have many sweet babies. Tell me what danger threatens.'

'There is going to be a terrible,' said the pelican. 'Soon no more water will flow from the mountains. The waterfall will cease to tumble and this pool will dry up to nothing. Then, I am sorry to have to tell you, you and your young ones will die.'

Ruan the fish was alarmed at this news. He did not stop to think that the waterfall was tumbling as strongly and as noisily as it ever had. He did not consider that, if indeed there had been a drought, the flow of water would already be slowing.

No, he swam in circles and wailed, 'What will become of my dear children? What will become of my loving wife? What will become of me?'

'How can I ignore the cries of such a dutiful parent!' sighed the pelican. 'I will help you, if you wish.'

'Can you? Will you? I will always be grateful to you,' puffed Ruan the fish.

'I have travelled the world,' said the pelican. 'I know many

things. I know the way to a pool, that is fed by a deep spring. In the worst drought that pool never runs dry. I will carry you and your family to this place of safety. You can see that my beak is large and comfortable. Will you snuggle into it and make the journey?'

'Oh, indeed, indeed we will!' gasped Ruan. 'A friend such as you is beyond price.'

'I will take you first to show you the beauty of your new home,' said the pelican and, opening his mouth, he waited for Ruan the fish to jump in.

Eagerly Ruan flipped his tail and leaped out of the water. His head spun as he swayed to and fro in the suffocating darkness of the pelican's beak.

The pelican walked a few paces round a corner of the hillside to a pool further down the same river. It could have been a journey of a hundred miles for all Ruan knew in his flurry of excitement.

FLOP! The pelican opened its mouth and let Ruan slide into the cool water.

'Wonderful!' gasped the fish, when he had recovered his senses. 'You have found a new home of exquisite beauty for me and my wife and little ones. Please take me back to them, so that I can prepare them for their removal.'

Once more the pelican opened his beak and then carried Ruan the fish the few paces to his old home.

'Hurry! Hurry! Prepare for a long journey,' called Ruan, twisting through the water and calling his family away from where they were safely feeding. 'Soon this pool will dry up. Our lives are in terrible danger, but a wonderful new friend will carry us to a beautiful new home.'

His wife and young ones were confused at this startling news, but after a while they gathered their wits together and swam up to the edge of the water.

'I will go first and wait for you in the new pool,' said Ruan.

'Of course! Of course!' replied his wife and children. 'Look out for the best feeding places. Find where the shadows fall so that we can keep out of the sun.'

They had never been so excited before. The pelican bent down and, catching Ruan in his beak, carried him to the pool around the corner of the hillside.

Ruan didn't see the pelican again. He looked for good places to feed and found where the shadows fell across the new pool. He

waited at the edge of the water for his family to join him, but he was disappointed. No one came.

He flapped anxiously from side to side, asking the fish in the new pool if they had seen any youngsters arriving. They had not, and nor had they heard talk of any drought. Ruan began to have the most terrible doubts.

Meanwhile, the pelican was taking Ruan's little ones, one by one, from the old pool under the waterfall. Instead of carrying them to the new pool, the pelican was swallowing them into its pouch.

'Who is next?' called the pelican each time he returned to the waterside.

'Me! Me! Take me next!' called the baby fish, pressing eagerly forward and showing that they were true children of their father.

When all the fish were in its pouch, the pelican turned his eyes towards the crabs, who lived in the same pool by the waterfall. He told them the same story about the drought and how the pool would soon be dry.

'Really! How very interesting!' said the oldest and biggest crab. 'Bend down and tell me more.'

Now crabs are quite different from fish. They can walk from the water to the land and back again. They travel the world and they see things and they learn from what they see. The oldest and biggest crab had already concluded that if the water was still pouring over the waterfall as strongly as ever it had, then the story of the drought could not be true. He had also decided that the pelican was a creature that the inhabitants of the pool could well manage without.

The pelican bent down to tell the crab about the wonderful pool fed by the ever-flowing spring to which he could carry him. Before the pelican could utter any more of his lies, the crab seized him round the throat and squeezed with his pincers until the pelican was dead. The bird's beak fell open and all the little fish and their mother swam out to safety in their old pool.

The only person to suffer any harm from the whole affair was the pelican himself. Even silly Ruan had the sense to swim out of his new pool and back up the river to his old pool. There he was re-united with his family and went back to pretending he was a mottled brown stone.

9
Into the Jungle

The Malay peninsula swings south-east into the China Sea and breaks up into a necklace of islands: Sumatra, Java, Bali, Sumbawa, Flores, Timor, Tanimbar and so east to New Guinea and the Pacific. Some of these islands are densely populated and many tales of princes and princesses have come from them.

A handsome prince named Sedana was brought up with his beautiful cousin, Princess Scri, in her father's palace. The cousins loved each other and hoped that when they grew up they would marry.

It was the custom in those days for young men approaching manhood to be sent into the jungle to live with a holy man. There they were taught to understand man's insignificance in the face of eternity. They learned humility, and that man must accept his fate. The time came for Prince Sedana to go off into the jungle to study these things.

Meanwhile, reports of Princess Scri's beauty spread throughout the land. Many kings wished to marry her, but no marriage was arranged because Princess Scri was waiting for her beloved Sedana to return from the jungle. Princess Scri's father approved of the match and so their happiness seemed assured.

One day the great and warlike King Pulagra heard of Princess Scri's beauty and wanted to marry her. 'I am the greatest King,' he roared. 'So I must marry the most beautiful princess.'

He sent his most ferocious warrior, Kalendra, to ask for Princess Scri's hand in marriage.

Kalendra strode into the palace with his sword clinking at his side, accompanied by fierce bodyguards.

'I am sorry,' said Princess Scri's father, 'but the Princess is already betrothed.'

'Break the betrothal,' said Kalendra in a soft voice. His appearance was so terrifying that he did not need to shout.

The King, Princess Scri's father, shook with fright as he walked to the rooms of the ladies of the court. His face was ashen as he sat down to speak to his wives and daughter.

'There is a madman with a sword standing in front of my throne!' he gasped. 'He wants Scri to marry King Pulagra!'

He turned to the Princess. 'Pulagra is a great and wealthy King, he is a good match. Consent to marry him and save all our lives.'

Princess Scri hesitated. 'What is King Pulagra like?' she asked. 'Is he young? Is he handsome? Is he good-natured and agreeable? Is he anything like my dear cousin, Prince Sedana?'

'He has a big army,' replied her father. 'That is all that need concern us.' The King knew, as did his wives, that King Pulagra was old and grey, with grown-up children.

Princess Scri shook her head. 'I do not wish to marry anyone but Sedana,' she said. 'I will wait for him to return.'

No matter how her father and his wives begged, Princess Scri would not change her mind. The King was furious.

'You have no choice,' he said. 'I have no choice. Even if Prince Sedana came back from the jungle, he would have little chance against this warrior. Kalendra is in our palace now with a drawn sword in his hand. We cannot say "No".'

The King went back to Kalendra. 'The unexpectedness of the proposal has overwhelmed Princess Scri,' he said. 'Please rest for the night and we will speak again in the morning.'

During the night the Princess escaped from the palace and fled into the jungle, looking for her dear Prince Sedana.

'Ungrateful girl!' raged her father. 'All I can do now is try to save those of us she has so callously left behind.'

Too frightened to face the ferocious Kalendra himself, the King sent his chief courtier. 'My dearest daughter, whom I willingly give as wife to King Pulagra, is too young to realise what is best for her,' ran the message. 'She has fled into the jungle. There are many paths in the jungle, and I do not know which way she has gone. If Kalendra wishes to use his renowned skills to find her, he has my permission to take her back to the court of King Pulagra for the marriage to take place.'

This cringing message had its desired effect. Kalendra left the court without killing anyone or destroying anything, and he marched off into the jungle to look for Princess Scri.

The Princess had many hours start and had walked for a long way. She had asked for shelter at the home of an old man and his wife who grew rice for a living.

The distance was nothing to Kalendra. He followed the tracks of the Princess until he came to the home of the rice farmers. He kicked the door off its hinges, strode into the middle of the room and held up his sword, letting the sunlight glint on its razor sharpness. 'Where is the Princess?' he asked with a sweet smile.

The poor old farmer and his wife were loyal to their Princess and denied seeing her. They said they would not know a Princess if they saw one. In any case the well-dressed young lady had told them quite clearly that she was not a princess. Kalendra tied the old man to one of his own jack-fruit trees and searched the house. He did not find the Princess. She had slipped out through the back door as the warrior had kicked his way in through the front.

Meanwhile the gods in heaven were disturbed by all the noise. The great god Batara Guru sent his brother Nerada down to earth to help Princess Scri. 'Show her the way to Prince Sedana,' he commanded.

Princess Scri ran towards the humble hut where her cousin was studying. He was surprised to see her and amazed at her distress. When she told him her story, he looked doubtful.

'Perhaps it would be better if you married King Pulagra,' he said. 'Perhaps it is not our fate that we should wed. How can we be sure of anything in the face of the mysteries of eternity?'

This was not the greeting the Princess had expected.

'Of course we should be together,' she snapped, 'it was Nerada, the messenger of Batara Guru himself, who guided me to your hut. Now prepare yourself for battle because Kalendra, the great warrior, will soon be here.'

She had hardly finished speaking to him when the door was flung back and light came blazing into the dim hut. There stood Kalendra. He seized Princess Scri by the arm, and told Sedana that he had her father's permission to take her to be married to

King Pulagra. Drawing himself up to his full glittering height, he smiled down at Sedana. 'Everything has been done correctly,' he said. 'Surely you do not wish to make trouble?'

Prince Sedana had been taught by the holy man to consider every man's opinion fairly. He hesitated, for he could see no flaw in Kalendra's argument. Then he looked at his beautiful cousin and found the reason to fight.

Luckily the gods were still watching. Nerada was sent to earth again. He thrust a magic arrow into Sedana's hands and with its help, Kalendra was put to flight. The great Kalendra had been defeated with the help of the gods.

But Prince Sedana could offer no comfort to his cousin. 'We have defeated Kalendra,' he said, 'but what shall we do now? If we go to live with your father, King Pulagra will send his army to attack him. He will attack anyone with whom we seek shelter.'

'Then we must live in the jungle on our own,' replied Princess Scri. 'We can grow our own food on this fertile land.'

'You mean work like farmers?' gasped Prince Sedana in dismay. 'When shall I have time to learn? The mysteries of the universe have not yet been revealed to me. I must spend many more hours gazing into my inner soul before I attain peace with myself.'

'The gods are with us,' replied Princess Scri. 'There will be time for everything.'

The Prince and Princess cleared the land. They obtained seeds and tools from friendly farmers and built a garden and a home for themselves in the jungle.

Then Princess Scri remembered the old man and woman who had helped her and she sent Prince Sedana to see if they were all right. He found them in despair because their house was destroyed, so he invited them to live with him and the Princess in their new home.

'Give your own land to your children,' he said. 'Come and help me grow food in our new home, deep in the jungle.'

The old couple went with him and they all prospered.

Meanwhile Kalendra had recovered from his injuries. He went back to King Pulagra and told him what had happened. The King gathered his army and marched in search of the Prince and Princess. His men plundered and destroyed everything in their path, as a warning to others never to oppose the greatest King in the land. The gods in heaven were disturbed once again.

'All that noise and dust and shouting!' groaned the great god, Batara Guru. 'It is frightful!'

He glared at some of the lesser gods. 'Go down to earth and stop this turmoil at once,' he ordered, 'and arrange matters so that it does not start again.'

Five lesser gods snatched up their weapons and flew down to earth. They fought a fierce battle with King Pulagra's army and at last they defeated it. The King went back to his kingdom and did not bother the other kings of the island again.

Then the five gods went in search of Princess Scri and Prince Sedana. 'This matter must be resolved,' they ordered. 'A marriage must take place.'

'But whose marriage and to whom?' asked the Prince. 'Would it be best for the peace of the country if Princess Scri were to marry King Pulagra? Is it selfish for us to wish to marry each other? Would it be wise for the Princess to marry King Pulagra when she does not love him? Would her unhappiness make him unhappy and bring trouble to our people? Would our happy marriage produce a wise son, who would be the greatest blessing to the island? Is such an idea wishful thinking?'

The five gods held up their hands. 'Do you wish to marry Princess Scri or not?' they asked.

'I wish to marry someone exactly like her,' replied the Prince, 'but is it the will of fate that I should marry her? Who knows?'

The gods looked at the Princess. 'Do you wish to marry Prince Sedana?' they asked.

'I wish to marry someone exactly like him,' replied Princess Scri, who had begun to think like the Prince, 'but whether, in the judgement of eternity, I should be selfish to insist on marrying this particular man, I do not know.'

'We order you to marry each other,' said the five gods, as if they were one person. So the marriage took place and there was peace on the island.

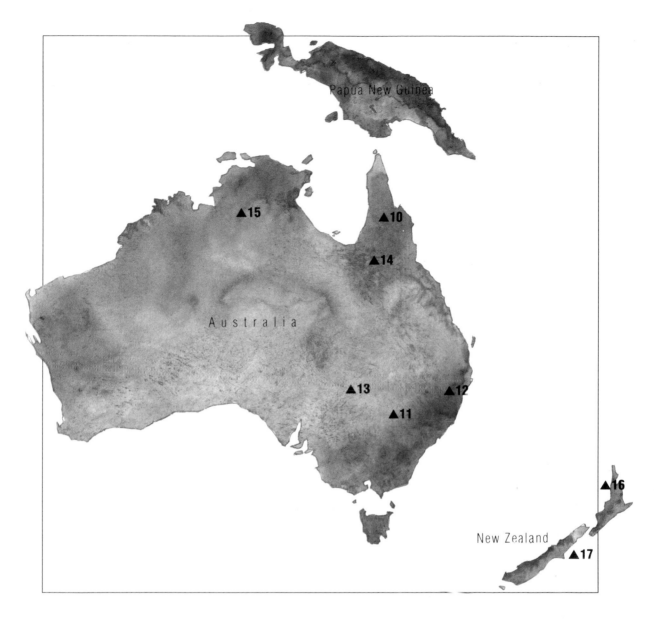

Australia and New Zealand

10 How the Dingo came to Australia

11 How the Sun was made

12 The Firemakers

13 Wirreenum the Rainmaker

14 Rainbow Serpent

15 Deereeree and the Rainbow

16 Maui the Fisherman

17 Kahukura and the Fishing Nets

10

How the Dingo Came to Australia

The Aborigines of Australia have lived in that vast country for more than 40,000 years and their legends have been handed down from generation to generation. Most Aborigine legends are concerned with the natural world – the origin of the sun, the making of fire and the habits of birds and animals. The Dreamtime was the mystic time during which the Aborigines' ancestors established their world.

Long ago in the Dreamtime, there was an old Grasshopper woman called Eelgin. She travelled with a giant devil-dingo named Gaiya. Gaiya was as big as a horse and ferocious, but he did as the Grasshopper woman told him. The two of them hunted people and ate them for food.

One day Eelgin, the Grasshopper woman, went to live on Cape York. She made a camp and built her humpy hut from scrub and branches. She thought she had come to a fine place. She thought so even more when she saw the Chooku-chooku boys walking by. They were Butcher-bird brothers and they were well fed.

'You are welcome to camp here for the night, boys,' called Eelgin, the Grasshopper woman, thinking that when the devil-dingo returned he would be able to kill the boys for her dinner.

The brothers glanced round uneasily. There was something about Eelgin they did not like. Then they saw the footprints of the giant devil-dingo. 'We will go on our way,' they replied.

As soon as they were out of sight of Eelgin, the Chooku-chooku boys took to their heels and ran away fast. They were wise to do so. Some hours later Gaiya returned to Eelgin's camp.

'Trust you not to be here when I wanted you,' screeched the old woman. 'Two delicious-looking boys walked by when the sun was still high in the sky. They would have made a tasty dinner for both of us, but, of course, you were hunting somewhere else.'

Eelgin scowled at the giant devil-dingo, who had caught nothing. 'I'll show you their trail,' she said. 'You catch those boys and bring them back or you'll be sorry.' The Grasshopper woman pointed to the tracks left hours before by the Butcher-bird brothers. The giant devil-dingo sniffed their scent and followed in rapid pursuit.

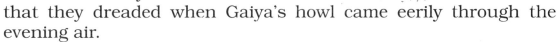

Meanwhile, the Chooku-chooku boys were still running away as fast as they could. Then they heard the sound that they dreaded when Gaiya's howl came eerily through the evening air.

The boys ran and hid, ran and then hid, day after day. They were fit and strong and they had a good start, but the dingo was huge and hungry. At last the boys knew without a doubt that they would soon be overtaken.

'Our only chance is to lie in ambush and spear him before he can attack us,' said one brother, and the other agreed.

They ran on until they found a pass through the hills near Barrow Point where the sides were rocky and covered with scrub. The Chooku-chooku boys agreed that one should hide on the right of the pass while the other lay in wait on the left.

Tired and breathless, the Butcher-bird boys scrambled up the hillside. They could still hear the terrifying howling of the giant devil-dingo behind them, and now they could also feel the vibrations of his huge paws thudding on the ground. The boys fingered their spears and waited, wondering if these moments would be their last. A lolling red shape entered the valley.

'Here he is! Spear him quickly!' shouted the younger boy.

'That is his tongue. Spearing that will not kill him,' replied his brother. 'Wait!'

Then a huge, hairy, brown triangle with two glowing red slots in it came rising and falling between the rocks.

'Spear him, before it is too late,' screamed the younger boy.

'No! That is his head and those slits are his eyes. Wait for a better target!' shouted the elder brother.

Then the rippling, loping shoulders of the giant devil-dingo came into sight. The elder brother started to throw his spears. First one, then another pierced the furry side of the fearsome pursuer. The dingo stumbled and fell.

The younger brother rushed forward and speared the dingo from the other side. At last the mighty Gaiya was dead.

All the while the Grasshopper woman, old Eelgin, was hobbling along on the trail of her pet, hoping for a fine dinner.

The Chooku-chooku brothers were delighted with their kill. They called all the people of their tribe to come and cut up the giant dingo and divide the meat.

Woodbarl, the medicine man, touched the elder brother on the arm. 'The spirit of the devil-dingo lives in the tail,' he warned.

The boy struck the tail from the body with one slash of his knife. 'Now go back to meet the Grasshopper woman,' he said to the spirit. 'I hear her hobbedy-hobbling along on your trail. See what she thinks of your hunting today. Tell her to send no more devil-dingos to catch the Butcher-bird brothers.'

The spirit of Gaiya ran back along the trail. Eelgin saw him coming. 'Did you catch those delicious boys?' she asked.

The spirit growled ferociously and bit Eelgin on the nose. 'You deserve that for sending me after those two boys who killed me,' he snarled.

Gaiya's carcass was divided up between the tribe according to custom. The medicine man took the kidneys and the head, as was his right. 'Give me the bones and skin too,' he said. 'The giant devil-dingo must walk the land no more, but a good dog would be useful.'

The medicine man went to the top of a high mountain. He rolled the kidneys, head, bones and skin together and made a male and female dingo. He made them small, so that they could not threaten man. Then he blew into their mouths and breathed life into them. The two new creatures stood up and howled. It was not the roaring howl of Gaiya; it was the small howl of a brave little friend, who would follow at the heels of man.

When this was done, the Chooku-chooku brothers went to find Eelgin, the Grasshopper woman. They found her sitting by the trail, clutching her bitten nose. They sharpened their spears and killed her. They glared at her spirit as it came out of her body and said, 'You stay at Barrow Point.' And she did.

Later on, when the Dreamtime ended, the Chooku-chooku boys turned into real butcher-birds. Eelgin's descendants became true grasshoppers, and the mark of Gaiya's bite still shows on their noses. You have only to look at a grasshopper's nose to see the truth of that.

11

How the Sun Was Made

Long ago in the Dreamtime, before there were men on earth, there was no sun in the sky. A dim light came from the moon and the stars, and the birds and animals down on earth had to creep about in the gloom as best they could.

One day Dineewan the emu and Brolga the crane met on a large plain near the Murrumbidgee River. They started quarrelling and fighting, no one knows why, but they were in a great rage with each other.

Suddenly Brolga ran to Dineewan's nest and snatched one of the huge eggs. With all her strength she flung the egg high into the sky. Up and up it soared until it was far too high to fall down again. Then it burst, and the yolk landed on a heap of firewood and set light to it. The fire blazed red and gold, and cast light on the plain below. The animals were amazed. Their eyes were dazzled but they were pleased – for the first time they could clearly see the world about them.

Up in the sky, a good spirit noticed how much better it was on the earth below when there was light. He decided that the fire should be kindled every day to light up the world and make the lives of the animals happier.

All night long the spirit in the sky and his helpers collected wood and, as the next day was due to begin, the spirit was ready to light the huge fire. However, he thought it best to warn the creatures on the earth below, in case they should be frightened.

The spirit sent the morning star to shine and warn everyone on earth that the sun was about to blaze. But very few creatures were awake to notice the morning star gleaming in the sky. Most birds and animals slept on undisturbed.

The spirit turned to Gougourhgah, the kookaburra. 'Your loud braying laugh should rouse the soundest sleeper,' said the spirit. 'Will you wake up every morning, as the morning star shines, but before the sun begins to burn? Will you call with all of your voice's power? Will you screech "Gou-gour-gah-gah"?'

Gougourhgah the kookaburra agreed. He looked at the morning star shining in the sky. He looked at the huge fire waiting to be lit. He opened his big mouth and called, 'Gou-gour-gah-gah!'

Every creature on the plain near the Murrumbidgee River awoke. The great fire in the sky was kindled. At first the light was faint, then the flames grew stronger and hotter. At midday, the sun was ablaze, sending light and heat down on to everything below. Towards the end of the day, the blaze died away until only embers remained to make the pink and yellow glow of sunset. Then the good spirit in the sky wrapped the embers of the fire in clouds and preserved them.

The next morning he used the embers to light another fire, and so he has continued from that day to this.

As for the kookaburra, he continued to call 'Gou-gour-gah-gah,' before each dawn. Children were forbidden to laugh at his big mouth and his strident cry.

'If you insult Gougourhgah the kookaburra, he might stop calling and the sun might not shine in the sky,' the mothers told their children.

If children defied their mothers and ran behind Gougourhgah shouting 'Gou-gour-gah-gah' and laughing, then an extra tooth grew above their eye teeth. The children were disfigured and lost their beauty and everyone knew that they had laughed at Gougourhgah.

12

The Firemakers

Long ago, soon after the days of the Dreamtime, the tribes did not know how to make fire. They had to eat their food raw, or dry it in the heat of the sun.

In those days Bootoolgah, the crane, was married to Goonur, the kangaroo rat. One day Bootoolgah sat rubbing one stick against another. To and fro he rubbed the sticks, staring into the shimmering heat and thinking of nothing. Suddenly he noticed a smell of burning and saw a whiff of smoke coming from the sticks. He called to Goonur.

'Look! Smoke!' he said. 'Wouldn't it be wonderful if we could make fire and cook our food!'

With the help of Goonur, Bootoolgah collected dried grass and bark. He continued to rub the sticks together. At last a spark fell on the grass and caught it alight. The grass burned the bark and soon a fire was blazing. Bootoolgah and Goonur were delighted. They cooked a fish that they had caught, and ate it. It was delicious, far tastier than the raw food that they were used to.

Bootoolgah and Goonur kept the fire in firesticks that they hid in the seeds of the Bingahwinguls. They always carried one firestick with them in a pouch of kangaroo skin. They told no one their secret because they wanted to keep the fire for themselves.

Whenever Bootoolgah and Goonur caught fish, or had meat to eat, they crept away into the bush and lit a fire and cooked it. Their meals were delicious, but still they did not share their secret with the other members of their tribe. Sometimes they took left-over food back into camp to eat later. Then, one day, a member of their tribe noticed that their fish looked quite different.

'What have you done to that fish?' he asked.

'Oh, we let it dry in the sun,' they replied.

'Sun-dried fish never looked like that,' said the man, but Bootoolgah and Goonur would give him no other answer.

Everyone started talking about the way the mysterious pair kept sneaking away whenever it was time to eat. Obviously they had a secret that they did not wish to share. Boolooral, the night owl, and Quarrian, the parrot, were ordered to follow and spy on them.

Sure enough, next time fish were caught, Bootoolgah and Goonur took their portion and went away into the scrub. Boolooral, the night owl, and Quarrian, the parrot, followed them. The bush was thick and, fearing that they would lose sight of their quarry, Boolooral and Quarrian flew into a tree. They saw Bootoolgah and Goonur stop in a little clearing.

Boolooral and Quarrian watched the couple take their firestick from the kangaroo pouch and gather grass, bark and sticks. They saw them blow on the firestick and make a great fire. When the fire had sunk to embers, they put the fish into the heat and

cooked it. It was a finer meal than the rest of the tribe had eaten.

Boolooral and Quarrian hurried back and told the others. Everyone wanted to eat the delicious cooked food. However, it was plain that Bootoolgah and Goonur had no intention of sharing the secret, so the tribe discussed how the fire could be stolen.

At last they decided to hold a corroboree – a great tribal gathering and feast – and to do all the sacred dances. They hoped that Bootoolgah and Goonur would be so excited that they would relax their guard on the pouch and the firestick.

All the arrangements for the corroboree were made. Beeargah, the hawk, was told to pretend at the last minute that he was ill. He was to lie around moaning, and keep a watchful eye on the pouch to see if he could steal it.

Everything went as planned. Bootoolgah and Goonur came into camp. Goonur carried the kangaroo pouch carefully over her arm. They sat down to watch the dancing and Beeargah, the hawk, lay near them. Beeargah curled up as if in pain, but he never took his eyes from the kangaroo pouch. Several times the pouch slipped from Goonur's arm but each time, as Beeargah was about to seize it, Goonur noticed that the pouch had fallen and picked it up again.

At last the dancers of the Bralgah came forward. They were the most exciting and the funniest of all. Goonur rocked with laughter and forgot all about the precious pouch over her arm. As she clapped her hands and rocked in time with the dancing, she let the pouch fall and Beeargah seized his chance. He snatched the pouch and cut it open with one slash of his knife. He took the firestick and ran. He set fire to as many bundles of grass and bark as he could before Goonur noticed her loss.

Suddenly Goonur missed the pouch from her side. She cried with dismay and leaped to her feet. She and Bootoolgah ran after Beeargah, but he kept ahead of them, lighting fires wherever he went. Goonur and Bootoolgah looked around them and saw fires everywhere. What was the use of chasing Beeargah? They gave up the chase and said no more. From then on all the tribe had fire and everyone ate the delicious cooked food.

13

Wirreenum the Rainmaker

Once there was a terrible drought. No rain fell and the grass withered and blew away. The animals died and the people were hungry. The young men of the Noongahburrah looked suspiciously at Wirreenum the Rainmaker and muttered among themselves.

'If Wirreenum has the power to make rain, then why doesn't he do so?' they asked. 'The earth is dry. The grass blows away and there is no seed to grind. The kangaroo and emu are dying, and the duck and the swan have flown away. Soon we will all die. If Wirreenum has the power to change all this, why doesn't he do something?'

They glared angrily at Wirreenum the Rainmaker. Wirreenum noticed all this, but he said nothing. Instead, all on his own, he went down to the waterhole. He took with him a willgo-willgo. This was a long stick ornamented at the top with white cockatoo feathers. He put the willgo-willgo into the waterhole with two big, smooth stones next to it. Usually he kept these stones safely in a pouch because they were magical and had to be hidden from women.

For three days running, Wirreenum went to the waterhole and put in a willgo-willgo decorated with white cockatoo feathers.

On the third day he said to the young men, 'Cut bark and build huts. Then take ant-beds and build them a foot high and put wood for fires on top of them.'

The young men did as they were told.

Then Wirreenum called the whole tribe together and took them to the waterhole. He told everyone to plunge into the water and stay there until they were shivering with cold. Wirreenum plunged into the water with the others and went round to all of the young men pretending to bite a cinder from the head of each of them.

When he was shivering with cold, Wirreenum jumped from the water. All the other members of the tribe jumped out of the water

73

with him. They were exhausted and the young people went to sleep in the huts that they had built. The old people stayed awake to watch for the storm that they knew would come.

Black clouds rolled across the sky. Thunder shook the earth and lightning flashed. Everyone was terrified. The old people and the dogs crowded into the huts with the young ones. The men said nothing, the women wailed and the dogs whimpered.

Then Wirreenum went out and spoke to the storm. He sang to it and told it to keep away from the camp. After that the thunder and lightning drifted away. A chill breeze shivered the trees and the first rain began to fall. The rain fell in torrents and Wirreenum hurried to the waterhole and took away the long sticks and the two stones because they had done their work.

The whole country became green again and the tribe was saved. The men were so happy that they decided to hold a big corroboree, with dancing and feasting, to celebrate the end of the drought.

Remembering how the young men had doubted him, Wirreenum wanted to show off more of his power. He told the young men to invite the rainmaker from a nearby tribe to join them. When the man came, Wirreenum took him and all the men to Googoorewon, which was then a dry plain. The two rainmakers worked together and, with their double power, managed to fill the plain with water and turn it into a huge lake.

The young men were amazed, but still Wirreenum was not satisfied. 'Fish in the lake,' he said.

The young men laughed. 'There are no fish in rainwater,' they replied. 'That lake has not been made by water from rivers. There are no fish to be caught.'

'Fish in the lake,' insisted Wirreenum.

In order to please the rainmaker the young men fished. To their surprise they caught goodoo, murree, tucki and bunmillah. Now they really admired Wirreenum's powers, and he was satisfied.

'We are very fortunate indeed,' said the elders of the tribe. 'We will hold a bora to celebrate.'

A great bora ceremony to initiate the boys into manhood was held on a ridge of the mountains, far away from the women. The tribe rejoiced that there was now enough water and food for everyone.

14
Rainbow Serpent

Long ago in the Dreamtime, everything was different from the way it is now. The land was flat, and there were no rivers or lakes. There were no animals, only people. There was the earth and the sky and the sun and the rain. Sometimes, after the rain, a great rainbow of beautiful colours arched through the heavens.

One day the rainbow spirit turned himself into a serpent and came slithering down to earth. He landed at the very northernmost point of Australia.

I must find my own people, thought the Rainbow Serpent. I must find the people who speak the tongue I understand and who dance the steps that please me.

Rainbow Serpent twisted and slithered south across Cape York, where he made a big red mountain and called it Narabullgan. He crept close to the camp fires and listened to the tribes talking, but he could not understand a word and their voices were harsh in his ears. These cannot be my people, he thought. I must travel further south.

Rainbow Serpent was big and heavy and his weight made a deep gorge as he wriggled along. He travelled for many days. Every now and then he paused and raised his head and turned his ears to the wind. He heard laughter and chatter blowing down the breeze, but he never heard a word that he could understand.

Onwards went Rainbow Serpent, grooving out streams and valleys as he struggled along. He built two more mountains. One was made of hard granite; the other was soft and full of caves.

By this time Rainbow Serpent had reached Fairview, but still he had not found his own people. He was losing weight and the ground was becoming harder, so that the valleys he made as he slithered along were not so deep.

On and on he travelled until, to his delight, he heard singing and understood the words. His body swayed to the rhythm. These must be my people, he thought.

Rainbow Serpent crept closer and closer to the familiar sounds. A bora was taking place at a fine, big camp site by the meeting of two rivers. The people of the tribe were dancing and singing.

For a while Rainbow Serpent lay and watched. Then he spoke

to his people: 'I am Rainbow Serpent come out of the Dreamtime,' he said. 'You are my people.'

The tribe welcomed Rainbow Serpent and he lived among them. Rainbow Serpent taught his people many things. He showed them how to dance more gracefully and he taught them how to paste up their hair with beeswax. He gave them feathers to put on their heads and bones for their noses, and he painted white patterns on their bodies.

Everyone was happy that Rainbow Serpent had slithered down from the sky to join them and the tribe prospered.

Then the sky filled with black rain clouds, so the people built humpy huts and crawled into them to shelter from the wet. Two boys, who had been out hunting and had not built a humpy, ran into camp as the storm started.

'Give us shelter!' they called. 'Give us shelter!'

No one would let the boys in to share a humpy, not even Rainbow Serpent who was tired and snoring. The rain fell harder and harder and the boys became desperate.

'Give us shelter, someone!' they yelled. 'Make room for us somehow!'

At that Rainbow Serpent opened his mouth very wide so that it looked like the entrance to a warm red humpy hut. 'Come in here,' said Rainbow Serpent. 'You may shelter with me!'

Blinded by water running into their eyes, the boys ran into Rainbow Serpent's mouth and he swallowed them.

Rainbow Serpent began to worry that the tribe would guess what had happened to the boys and that the people might not like him any more. So he crept away north to the only mountain in that vast flat land.

Next morning the people were very surprised to find that their bright new friend, Rainbow Serpent, had left them. Then they asked after the two boys.

'There was no room for them in my humpy,' said one, 'did they take shelter in yours?'

'No,' was the reply. 'My humpy was filled with me and my children. I could not squeeze the boys in.'

When all the tribe had been questioned, the people guessed that Rainbow Serpent had eaten the two boys. The men picked up their spears and set off in pursuit. Rainbow Serpent could only move slowly because his stomach was heavy with his shameful meal. They easily followed his tracks.

Eventually they found Rainbow Serpent coiled round the top of Bora-bunara mountain. The Emu man, the Turkey brothers, Possum and many others all tried to climb up the mountain, but it was too steep for them.

At last two Tree Goanna brothers walked by to see what was causing all the commotion.

'Rainbow Serpent has eaten two of our boys, but we cannot climb up to rescue them,' said Emu.

The two Tree Goanna brothers fingered their quartz knives and said, 'We will climb up and save them for you.'

For several days and nights the two men climbed the mountain. Luckily for them Rainbow Serpent was deep in sleep, tired after his long journey across Australia.

Closer and closer scrambled the Tree Goanna brothers, until they reached the giant serpent. Then they slit through his skin with their sharp quartz knives and released the two boys. But the boys were no longer human: they had turned into lorikeet birds and their feathers were now the same lovely hues as Rainbow Serpent's skin. Flapping their wings, the boys flew down over their people and then soared away, glistening in the sunshine.

The Tree Goanna brothers came down from the mountain and told the tribe that the boys had been saved, but they had changed into birds. Everyone was pleased and they were about to go home, when they heard something stirring at the top of the mountain.

A cold wind had blown into Rainbow Serpent's mouth and woken him up. Looking down, he saw the wound in his side and realised that the two boys had escaped.

Rainbow Serpent was furious. How ungrateful! He had done so much for his chosen tribe and they repaid him by injuring him and robbing him of his dinner.

The great serpent swished his great tail from side to side and flashed his forked tongue in and out of his huge mouth. He broke up the huge mountain and sent pieces of it flying all over the countryside to make the many smaller mountains that can be seen today.

All the people were terrified. Some ran away swiftly and were safe. Others were so frightened that they themselves turned into animals and crept into holes in the ground; or they turned into birds and flew away through the sky; or they turned into insects and hid under stones. They did anything to escape the anger of Rainbow Serpent.

Rainbow Serpent filled the air with lightning and thunder and flying boulders, until the whole mountain was flattened. Then, hot and exhausted, he slid into the sea, where he lives to this day.

Behind him on the land, nothing was ever the same again. Now there were hills and valleys and lakes and rivers. There were fewer people, but many animals of all sizes and shapes. They all had to learn to live together.

Sometimes the people looked up into the sky and saw a bright shooting star. 'That is Rainbow Serpent's eye. It has flown up into the heavens to watch what we are doing,' they would say.

15

Deereeree and the Rainbow

Deereeree was a widow who lived in a lonely camp with her four daughters. One day Bibbee arrived and made his camp nearby. Deereeree was afraid because she was alone with four little girls. She lay awake all night long listening for sounds from Bibbee's camp. At the slightest noise Deereeree wailed with fear.

'Wyah, wyah, Deereeree, Deereeree,' she moaned loudly all night long.

The sound disturbed Bibbee and in the morning he went to Deereeree's camp to ask what was wrong.

'I am afraid,' said Deereeree. 'I thought I heard someone walking about in the night.'

'I heard no one,' replied Bibbee. 'There is nothing to fear.'

Bibbee returned to his camp. The next night he was disturbed again. From Deereeree's camp the wails of 'Wyah, wyah, Deereeree, Deereeree,' could be heard all night long.

Night after night Deereeree lay awake listening for sounds from Bibbee's camp. If she heard a noise of any sort, she thought there was danger and she would cry, 'Wyah, wyah, Deereeree, Deereeree.'

Bibbee again went to see her. 'If you are afraid,' he said, 'marry me. Come to live in my camp and I will protect you.'

Deereeree did not want to marry again and she refused. So things continued, with Deereeree lying awake, shaking with fear and crying out, while Bibbee was disturbed in his sleep. Many times Bibbee asked Deereeree to marry him, but always she refused.

At last Bibbee decided to impress Deereeree with his power so that she would be obliged to marry him. He made a beautiful rainbow that he called Euloowiree. It stretched from one side of the earth to the other, and it had many beautiful colours. It was a pathway that stretched up to the stars. Bibbee made Euloowiree, then he sat in his camp and waited.

When Deereeree woke up she saw the rainbow arching right

81

across the sky. She had never seen such a thing before and was terrified. She seized her four girls and ran to Bibbee's camp to ask for protection.

'There is no need to be afraid,' said Bibbee. 'I made Euloowiree the rainbow. It is beautiful and will do no harm. Now you see how powerful I am and you must marry me. If you do not marry me, instead of making lovely rainbows, I will make things that are terrible and cruel, and then you will have cause to fear.'

Deereeree changed her mind at once and agreed to marry Bibbee. She lived in his camp with her four daughters and he protected them.

When Deereeree died, she was changed into a willy-wagtail that cried, 'Deereeree, wyah, wyah, Deereeree.'

16

Maui, the Fisherman

The Maori people are believed to be of Polynesian origin. Sometime during the twelfth century they travelled in their large canoes across the vast Pacific Ocean from Hawaii to New Zealand.

Many years ago, near the beginning of time, soon after the earth and the sky had been forced apart and the trees had found room to grow tall and the light had found space to shine, Maui was born. He was the fifth son of a beautiful woman named Taranga, but he arrived before his time and was weak and feeble.

Taranga should have killed him, but when she looked into his eyes she knew she could not harm him. So she cut off her long hair, wrapped it around the baby and cast the wailing bundle into the sea.

The baby rocked in the cradle of the waves and, as his wails turned to gurgles of contentment, the God of the Ocean took pity on him and cared for him as if he were his own son. With such a protector, Maui learned the secrets of the glittering waters and became half a god himself.

When he had grown into a youth, Maui said goodbye to the God of the Ocean and, leaving the cold depths of the sea, walked up through the warm shallows and on to the hot sand of the beach. There he met an old man called Tama who took the boy home to live in his hut.

Tama taught Maui the ways of men and the secrets of the animals. He taught him spells and the magic of his tribe.

Now that he was wise in the ways of the sea and the land, both half god and a man of magic, Maui said, 'I must go to my own people.'

Saying goodbye to Tama, Maui walked away across the sand dunes. He travelled for many miles before he arrived, tired and footsore, at a clearing where smoke was rising from a long house.

Among the people walking about was a tall, beautiful woman. It was Taranga.

Maui knew her at once. He walked up to her and said, 'Mother, here I am. I am your son.'

Taranga looked at him and, forgetting the weakly baby she had cast away so many years before, said, 'I have four sons and you are not one of them.'

'You have five sons,' replied Maui. 'I am the fifth, whom you wrapped in your hair and cast into the sea. I am Maui.'

Then Taranga knew that this stranger was her son. She took him into her arms and loved him with all her heart, and Maui lived once more with his real family.

The years went by. Maui and all his brothers married and had children, but Maui's wife was not content. She complained that her husband was lazy and did not catch enough fish.

'I am a magnificent fisherman,' protested Maui. 'I learned my skills from the God of the Ocean himself.'

'So you say,' replied Maui's wife, 'but you do not practise your skills very often. You go fishing for one day and bring back a magnificent catch, but then you lie in the sun for a week while your family starves.'

Maui's brothers were jealous of him ever since he returned

from the sea with grand stories of being half a god. They agreed with Maui's wife.

'You are lazy, Maui,' they jeered. 'We feel sorry for your wife and children. You say you are half a god. You are certainly only half a man!'

Stung by these insults, Maui was determined to show his brothers that he was the finest fisherman who had ever stepped into a canoe. He went away and secretly made a fishing hook from his grandmother's jaw-bone. This was one of the skills he had learned from the God of the Ocean. Then he polished it with the magic secrets taught to him by the old man, Tama.

Maui returned to his wife. 'Tomorrow I will go fishing with my brothers,' he announced.

She nodded and yawned, having heard such promises many times before.

Maui went to his brothers. 'Tomorrow we will go fishing together,' he said. 'You can catch food to fill your bellies, but I shall haul up something that will dazzle your eyes with wonder.'

His brothers laughed. 'Day-dreaming does not fill cooking pots,' they said. 'Ask your children if they would rather have a father who brings home food or one who wastes his breath with boasting.'

They went home grinning, but Maui hid his magical fishing hook in the folds of his clothes and smiled the smile of a man who knows the secrets of the gods.

The next day Maui went fishing with his brothers and, to their dismay, he told them to paddle far from shore.

'It is dangerous and useless to go such a long way from land,' they objected. 'The sea currents will carry us away and besides, the fish like the warm shallows.'

'Fish? Fish? Why should I, a half god, be content with catching fish?' laughed Maui. 'Paddle further from the shore. Paddle out into the deep sea so that we can see the mysteries of the gods.'

Maui's brothers were terrified, but they did not dare disobey him. They paddled their canoe further out over the swelling waves until they could no longer see the land.

Then Maui took from the folds of his clothes the fishing hook he had made from his grandmother's jaw-bone. He attached it to a line and cast it over the side of the canoe. As the fishing hook sank through the water, Maui's brothers huddled together and watched with terror filled eyes.

Maui felt no fear. He knew very well what was in the depths

below because he had walked the valleys and hills of the land beneath the sea in the days of his youth.

First Maui felt a slight pull on the hook, but he did not haul in the line. 'That is only a carved figure on a rooftop,' he smiled.

He shook the hook free and let it float further until it caught firmly in a doorway. Maui knew that the hook was caught in the doorway of the house that belonged to the son of the God of the Ocean.

'Now I will haul up my catch,' smiled Maui and, chanting one of the magic songs taught to him by Tama, he hauled with all his strength. He hauled with the strength of a man, and with the strength of a god, and with the strength of worldly magic.

The canoe rocked and swirled. Mud darkened the water and patches of grass floated on the waves. Still Maui pulled and heaved at the fishing line. The foundations of the home of the son of the God of the Ocean were so firmly fixed that, as the house came up to the surface, it dragged the bed of the sea up with it.

Up came the roof, up came the house, up came the land and, looking round, Maui's brothers found that their canoe was out of the water and resting on grass. Their eyes were dazzled with wonder, as Maui had said they would be.

Maui and his brothers stepped from their canoe. 'Wait here while I find the God of the Ocean. I want to speak with him and make my peace,' said Maui.

The brothers stared with amazement at the lovely land on which they so unexpectedly found themselves. No sooner was Maui out of sight than they began to quarrel about who should be king over this new land. They shouted and fought and stamped. They threw rocks and clumps of grass at each other.

Soon they had broken the land into two islands. The rocks they threw became mountains. The places where their feet stamped became lakes. The tufts of grass became little islands round the shore.

By the time Maui returned, his brothers had made New Zealand into the shape it is today, with its two big islands, its mountains and lakes and the small islands around the coasts. Because it was the land of New Zealand that Maui pulled up from beneath the waves on that sunny, far-off day.

17

Kahukura and the Fishing Nets

Kahukura, the great Maori war chief, woke in the night. He rose to his feet and cried, 'A vision has come to me. In my sleep the mists of time were pulled aside and my eyes looked into the bright future. I saw my tribe happy and prosperous. I saw my tribe greater than any other.

'At this wonderful vision my heart warmed with happiness. Then a great voice called to me. Such a majestic voice could only have come from the gods. The voice told me to go north to the land of the Rangiaowhia. It told me to go alone and in secret. It told me that if I obeyed these instructions, I would bring back a great blessing for my people.'

On the next day Kahukura, the war chief, prepared to set out alone for the land of the Rangiaowhia.

'You must not do this!' cried his warriors. 'Our enemies are in the north. You will be captured and slaughtered if you go alone. What will become of us if our leader lies bleeding in the dust?'

'I will go alone, but I will also go in secret as the great voice told me,' said Kahukura. 'I will pass like a shadow at midnight and my enemies will not see me. I will walk as silent as the sun on a stone and my enemies will not hear me. I will be safe and I will bring back a blessing to my tribe.'

But the warriors were still afraid for his safety. They watched Kahukura day and night. If he attempted to slip away to travel north, small bands of men followed after him. The gods had told Kahukura that he must travel alone, so there was nothing he could do but return home.

Kahukura stretched his arms out to the great world of nature all around him. 'Voice of my dreams, voice of the gods,' he cried. 'I will obey you. I will obey. Keep the great blessing safe for me and I will come alone and in secret to bring it back.'

Kahukura waited until his tribe were having a feast. The warriors were gathered together to dance the Haka, the throbbing

dance of war. He stood with his long lines of brave warriors, brandishing his spear and stamping his feet.

Kahukura chanted the Haka in his thrilling, deep voice and his warriors chanted with him. They swayed and stamped and shouted and saw nothing but visions of victory and the smiling faces of heroes from the past. They did not see Kahukura pull his cloak of feathers about him and slip away into the darkness.

Alone and in secret, Kahukura set off north towards the land of the Rangiaowhia.

He travelled at dusk, when his enemies were going to their beds, and in the half-light of dawn, before they had brushed the sleep from their eyes. He travelled unseen and unheard and, after many days, he reached the land of the Rangiaowhia.

One evening he stood among the trees and looked out at a long curving beach, where the sea washed high and low across the sand. He heard rustling and scratching and yet no creature moved on the beach. Then he saw that the sea was filled with thousands of fish coming in on the flowing tide. There were so many of them that they turned the sea silver. The noise he heard was the sound of their scales brushing against each other.

Were these fish the great blessing for his tribe? Kahukura wondered. He hid among the leaves of a flax bush and watched and waited.

After many hours, when Kahukura's head was nodding with sleep, he heard the sound of beautiful music. Peering sleepily

between the leaves of the flax bush, he saw many small canoes being drawn up on the beach. Small fair people with golden hair stepped out of the canoes. Kahukura had heard about these golden-haired people who came from the sea, but he had never seen them before.

They ran about laughing and talking together while the young women set out food. Kahukura noticed that two groups of men were hauling in something from the sea. After a lot of effort a bag filled with holes flopped up on to the beach. Water spilled out of it, but hundreds of fish remained inside. Kahukura was looking at a fishing net.

This must be the blessing that would make his tribe happy and prosperous Kahukura thought. If he could take one of these wonderful nets home to his people, the days of catching a few fish on a line would be gone for ever. His people would never be hungry again.

Kahukura watched from the middle of the flax bush. How could he gain possession of this blessing? How would he know how to use it or how to make another when it wore out?

He watched the men shake the fish from the net on to the beach. Then they killed and gutted them, and loaded them into the canoes. The nets were spread out along the sand and the women cleaned off the weeds and sticks.

Then Kahukura heard a laugh and a squeal. One of the girls, with a small basket in her hands, was running away from a group of boys who had been teasing her. She ran straight towards Kahukura, then hid among some bushes a few paces away. She smiled as she peered out at the boys who were searching for her.

She was so lovely that Kahukura fell in love with her at once. His gaze lingered on her. Then he glanced to the fishing nets that were spread out in the moonlight. He would take them as the blessing promised by the voice in his dream.

Rising to his feet, Kahukura gave a loud shout and all the golden-haired people turned to look at him. They started to panic because they were terrified of ordinary human beings. The lovely young girl stood up too, wanting to run to the canoes. But when she saw how close she was to Kahukura, she sank down into the bushes again. She was shaking with fear.

Meanwhile, her companions were running round in circles, trying to save their catch of fish, trying to pick up their nets, trying to save themselves. Kahukura strode towards them with his broad shoulders and rippling muscles shining in the hard white light of the moon. The golden-haired people leapt into their canoes and paddled away. The precious fishing net was left on the beach among the fish heads and scales.

Kahukura turned to look back at the beautiful golden-haired girl. She stared at the fine, strong figure of the war chief. He was so much more handsome and braver than the men of her own race that she fell in love with him at once.

The couple returned hand in hand to the land where Kahukura's people lived. They took the fishing net with them and the girl's basket with the tools for mending the nets and making new ones.

'I have returned with the blessing I was told about in my dream,' said Kahukura to his tribe. They had missed him very much and waited anxiously for his return.

He held up the fishing net.

'Here is the blessing that will make this tribe greater than any other.' He turned to the girl at his side. 'And here is the blessing that will make me happier than any other man in the land.'

Kahukura and the girl from the sea lived happily together for the rest of their lives and produced many golden-haired children.